This book belongs to:

. . . .

SIMON SPOTLIGHT
An imprint of Simon & Schuster Children's Publishing Division
1230 Avenue of the Americas
New York, New York 10020

Printed in the United States of America

The Busy World of Richard Scarry™

Richard Scarry's Best Holiday Books Ever

The Best Christmas Present Ever!

Simon Spotlight

It's Christmas Eve!
The Cat family is excited not only about Christmas,
but also because Mother Cat is expecting a baby!
"It's time to go to bed," Father Cat tells Huckle, Sally, and Lowly.

"Good night, Daddy!
Good night, Mommy!"
Sally and Huckle say.

"And good night to you
too, baby!" Lowly says to
Mother Cat's tummy.

Suddenly Mother Cat begins to feel strange.
"John," she says. "I think the baby is coming soon."
"Oh, my!" exclaims Father Cat. "What do we do?"

"Wait! I made a list of what to do," remembers Father Cat, searching his pockets.

"Here is the list!" says Father Cat. "First, get the car ready," he reads.

"Oh, no!" exclaims Father Cat. "The car is almost buried under the snow."

"On a night like this, I wish our car was a sleigh instead," he says.

Father Cat clears the snow from the driveway.

Good work, Father Cat!
The car is ready to go.
What is next on the list?

"Don't forget Mother Cat's
suitcase," reads Father Cat.
"*This* should be easier!"

"The suitcase is all packed
and ready to go," says
Father Cat, walking back
inside. "If only I could
remember where I put it!"

Father Cat looks for the
suitcase throughout the entire house,
from the cellar to the attic. Where can it be?

"Are you looking for this?" says Mother Cat, holding the suitcase.
"Thank you, Fiona!" Father Cat says. "Where was it?"
"Beside the front door," she replies. "Right where you left it two
weeks ago."

Nana Cat comes to look after the children while Mother and Father Cat go to the hospital.

"Don't worry! I will take good care of the kids," says Nana Cat.

"I'm sorry we won't be here to celebrate Christmas with the children!" says Mother Cat.

"Gee, I wish I had planned for *that* on my list," says Father Cat.

"Wait! I have an idea!" he exclaims. "Let's make a surprise for the children!"

Soon Mother and Father Cat are ready to leave. Drive carefully! The snowy roads are slippery!

Father Cat is in a hurry to get to the hospital.
"Take it easy, dear," says Mother Cat.

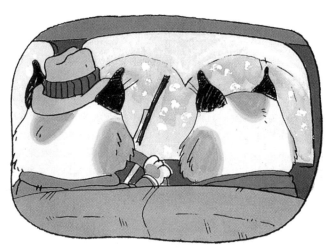

Suddenly the car skids out of control to the left . . .

Then to the right . . .
Whumpf!
The car plows into a snowbank and stops.
Oh, no, Father Cat!

"Are you okay, Fiona?"
Father Cat asks.
"I am fine," replies
Mother Cat. "But do
you think we can
get out?"

Father Cat tries to get the car back
on the road, but the wheels sink
deeper into the snow.
"Getting stuck was definitely not
on my list," Father Cat sighs.

What luck! Here comes Mr. Fixit in his tow truck! "Hello, Mr. Fixit!" Father Cat calls.

"Merry Christmas, Mr. and Mrs. Cat!" Mr. Fixit replies. "You look like you need some help!"

"Yes, thank you!" says Father Cat. "We need to get to the hospital, our baby is on its way!"

Vroom! Vroom!
Mr. Fixit backs up to the
Cat family car.

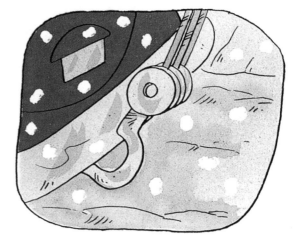

Clang!
Then Mr. Fixit hooks the
car to his tow truck.
Tada!

"Hop aboard, everyone!" exclaims Mr. Fixit.
Mother and Father Cat climb into Mr. Fixit's warm tow truck.

"You must be so excited to have a new baby!" Mr. Fixit says. "Thanks for your help! I am just hoping Dr. Lion can get to the hospital with all this snow," replies Mother Cat.

"I wouldn't worry about that," replies Mr. Fixit. "Look!"

Dr. Lion's car is also stuck in a snowbank!

It looks like he needs a lift too!

Thanks to Mr. Fixit's help, Mother and Father Cat and Dr. Lion arrive at the hospital on time. This is going to be a busy night—and not just for Santa!

It's Christmas morning!
Merry Christmas, everyone!
Sally, Huckle, and Lowly hurry
downstairs to find their presents.

But the living room is empty!
"What happened to our Christmas
tree?" Huckle asks.
"And where are all the presents?"
wonders Lowly.

"At least Santa came!" says Sally. "He filled our stockings!"

"But where are Mommy and Daddy?" wonders Huckle.

"Don't worry, children," says Nana Cat. "Your mommy and daddy have just gone to get a big Christmas surprise for you!"
"This is the weirdest Christmas ever!" Sally says.

After breakfast Nana Cat drives the children to see the surprise. Hmm . . . They aren't too pleased!

"What kind of surprise can you find in a *hospital*?" wonders Sally.

Nana Cat leads the children through the hospital.
"The surprise is behind this door," Nana Cat tells the children. "You may open it!"

"A baby!" Sally, Huckle, and Lowly exclaim.

"This is your new sister," Mother Cat tells the children.
"Babykins is her name!"
"WOW!" The children exclaim together.

"This has been a pretty strange Christmas," says Huckle.
"But this sure is the *best* Christmas present ever!"

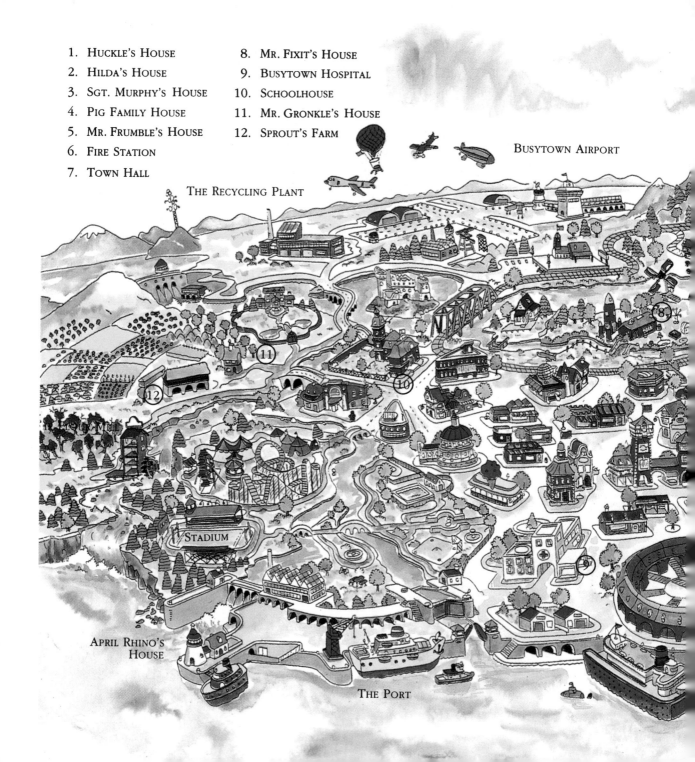

1. HUCKLE'S HOUSE
2. HILDA'S HOUSE
3. SGT. MURPHY'S HOUSE
4. PIG FAMILY HOUSE
5. MR. FRUMBLE'S HOUSE
6. FIRE STATION
7. TOWN HALL
8. MR. FIXIT'S HOUSE
9. BUSYTOWN HOSPITAL
10. SCHOOLHOUSE
11. MR. GRONKLE'S HOUSE
12. SPROUT'S FARM

BUSYTOWN AIRPORT

THE RECYCLING PLANT

STADIUM

APRIL RHINO'S HOUSE

THE PORT

MOUNT BUSY
OBSERVATORY

SKI CHALET

Welcome to Busytown!

CAMPING GROUNDS

BUSY BAY
POINT

BRUNO'S
SNACK
STAND

① ④ ② ③ ⑥

THE BEACH

THE
TRAIN
STATION

BUSYTOWN GRAND HOTEL

SEA FORT